Midnight Louie in
SOMETHING FISHY

*"The oldest and strongest emotion of mankind is fear,
and the oldest kind of fear is fear of the unknown."*

H. P. Lovecraft in his essay,
"Supernatural Horror in Literature"

Midnight Louie in
SOMETHING FISHY
(Iä Iä Iä-Iä Cthulouie!)

by **Carole Nelson Douglas**

Illustrated by Brad Foster
Introduction by Ed Gorman

A Midnight Louie Adventure[*]
(*after H. P. Lovecraft)

COZY NOIR BOOKS
Fort Worth · Texas

ISBN: 0-9744742-0-7
First separate edition: October 2003
First published in *Cat Crimes for the Holidays* (November 1997)

copyright ©2003 by Cozy Noir Press
Illustrations copyright ©2003 by Brad W. Foster
Introduction copyright ©2003 by Ed Gorman

All rights reserved. No part of this book may be reproduced in any means, electronic or mechanical, including photocopy, recording, or any information storage and retrieval system without prior written consent of the publisher.

First Cozy Noir Press edition 2003
10 9 8 7 6 5 4 3 2 1

Cozy Noir Press
PO BOX 331555
Fort Worth TX 76163-1555
http://www.catwriter.com

Printed in the United States of America

Text set in garamond
Book design/Margie Adkins West

For Sandie Herron, book and cat lover par excellence,
and a great friend to Midnight Louie and me,
and for her Fab Five, Big Block, Riley, Indy,
Tasha, and Zora, the luckiest cats in the world

And for Summer, the shaded silver Persian
and role model for the Divine Yvette

Introduction
by Ed Gorman

It has fallen to me to reveal one of the most insidious secrets of our time.

This one is so hot that even the supermarket tabloids are afraid of it. I have a special interest in the short story that reveals it. Not only is Carole Nelson Douglas one of my favorite people and favorite writers—I bought the story for its original publication.

The "secret" I'm referring to, of course, is the indisputable connection between a certain large black tomcat named Midnight Louie and an evil being called Cthulhu, which H.P. Lovecraft expert Daniel Harms has described as "a large green being . . . with the head of a squid, huge bat-wings, and long talons." Feel free to invite him over for dinner anytime.

Cthulhu now resides, according to Harms, on the bottom of the ocean where, in its sleep, it sends out telepathic messages to various human beings who, under its thrall, do terrible things. Think Richard Speck, Charles Manson, Ted Bundy, and the man who invented "reality TV."

Cthulhu (though he was actually named by writer August Derleth), was a creation of H. P. Lovecraft, a writer of horror who came into true prominence and importance only after his death.

During his lifetime, he was the subject of intense favor by a small group of readers and writers. The latter included such classic authors as Robert Bloch of *Psycho* fame, and the fantasists Fritz Leiber and Henry Kuttner, each of whom both imitated him and corresponded with him. Lovecraft's primary fictional outlet was a wonderful pulp magazine called *Weird Tales.*

What has always drawn me to Lovecraft is his dark explanation for all the calamity and suffering in the world. In some ways, he answers the timeless question of the poet Verlaine: "Why are we born to suffer and die?"

Well, according to Lovecraft, the universe is influenced, perhaps even controlled by the Great Old Ones, a sinister collection of deities who mean nothing but ill for humankind. Cthulhu is one such deity. Lovecraft offers horrible images to explain the inexplicable dread that so many people seem to feel. If we could see what is really around us, he seems to say, we would be driven mad, just as so many of his own characters were. Lovecraft's world is one of eternal night—even if the sun is shining—and the cold of the grave and of the worlds that lie beyond death.

Carole Nelson Douglas, one of today's most accomplished writers, and a happy, smiling, intelligent and supremely positive woman, has somehow fallen under old H.P.'s sway. She has taken one of her most popular creations—Midnight Louie, the feline private detective who helps narrate and solve Carole's Las Vegas cases (you can tell when Louie's on stage—he writes the bold-faced, interpolated chapters)—and set him in a situation that has obviously been inspired by the Lovecraftian world.

Except this time instead of Vegas, Louie's gone to that town Lovecraft warned all his readers about, Innsmouth, Massachusetts, to film a cat food commercial. There, he encounters strange religious ceremonies, dead people who aren't quite dead, and a creature one doesn't want to gaze upon too long—i.e., Midnight

Louie comes smack dab up against the work of Cthulhu.

Hi-jinks, hilarity and some moments of true horror ensue. This is a Midnight Louie tale unlike any other. So how did this come to be written and published here?

Here's what Carole has to say on the matter:

"This is the first Midnight Louie short story to be published in an illustrated edition. It debuted in one of the long-running "Cat Crimes" anthologies edited by Ed Gorman, in November of 1997.

"Being a black-cat detective, Louie was eager to contribute to *Cat Crimes for the Holidays* as long as he could chose his birthday: October 31 (naturally), a.k.a. Halloween.

Midnight Louie first appeared as a feline sleuth in a romantic suspense miniseries of four short novels for the Loveswept romance line. Commissioned in 1985, the books were not published until 1990 in a truncated form.

Midnight Louie, being a hard-boiled PI and a cat to boot, did not take kindly to truncation, editorial or otherwise. He was resurrected for his own series of mysteries in 1991, and recently celebrated the release of his 15th book in that series, *Cat in a Neon Nightmare.* The earlier quartet of books were released in author-revised and restored limited library editions from Five Star in 1999-2000, and are now out of print.

The following story brings Louie and his ladylove, the Persian he calls the Divine Yvette, to H. P. Lovecraft country: Innsmouth, Massachusetts. As Louie's collaborator, I've occasionally been accused of introducing a fantasy element to mystery. I proudly plead guilty, for I was a fantasy and science fiction author before I officially entered the mystery field. And before that, even before I was a fiction writer, I was an admirer of the works of H. P. Lovecraft, whom I consider the finest American fantasist and horror writer since Edgar Allen Poe."

A list of some of Lovecraft's collected works follows the story, in case readers would like to dip into more Lovecraftian tales to furthur explore his vast, original, and haunting fictional world.

But first, let's celebrate Halloween Louie's way. The call of *Iä Iä Hastur* often invokes the unearthly goings-on in a Lovecraft tale. The play on that phrase in the subtitle of this story makes clear that Midnight Louie is on the case and that this is a Lovecraftian tale like no other.

Ed Gorman
June, 2003

Chapter 1
The Call of À La Cat

W<small>HEN ALL</small> L<small>AS</small> V<small>EGAS</small> is your oyster, it is next to impossible to take a vacation. Where is there to go? It is all here. New York, New York, Monte Carlo, the Luxor hotel pyramid and sphinx, even the wacky world of Oz at the MGM Grand. Just name some place else and someone in Las Vegas will have recreated it on a scale that would make epic film director Cecil B. DeMille gnash his dentures with envy.

Nowadays the old town hypes its image with a television commercial. After a visual smorgasbord of the Strip's newest reconstructions, a voice-over boasts: "Las Vegas, it is like no place else."

Problem is, Las Vegas has become exactly like *every* place else. A dude can hardly scratch up any native sand on which to transact a bit of private personal business.

Still, Las Vegas is my beat, even if it looks more like a movie studio backlot these days, and I am fond of the old town in spite of all its grand and gaudy excesses. No place offers hot-and-cold running excitement on quite the scale of this multi-personality metropolis on the Mojave, so I am not enthused at the notion of leaving my native turf, even for a business trip, especially not at my signature holiday, Halloween.

1

"Think of it as a vacation, Louie," my normally doting room-mate, Miss Temple Barr, coos through my carrier grille. She is looking guilty, as well she should.

A white stretch limo that extends into next week purrs at the curb outside my home, sweet home, the Circle Ritz condominium and apartment building. Even though I am the original Dude in Black, twenty pounds of tooth and nail in an ebony fur coat, I am being crated and freighted into the hands of cinemactress Miss Savannah Ashleigh and a cat trainer for a flight to the country's opposite coast. My only consolation for this ignominy is that another carrier inside the limo's dark cocoon shelters my devoutly to be wished sweetheart, the Divine Yvette.

"Be good," Miss Temple croons, waving her little hand as I watch her slide away through a tinted glass window, darkly. I hope this is not an omen for the success of this holiday jaunt.

Although I could play the national poster boy for the holiday in question, Halloween is not usually a prime time for one of my species and color. Luckily, I am not your average pussycat, but a self-appointed feline detective now moonlighting as a jet-setting spokescat. I am no lightweight in any respect, a fact that they carp about at the airport when they hand-carry the Divine Yvette and myself to the gate.

The purebred Miss Divine, a Hollywood honey who keeps her weight at a petite seven pounds, travels in a pink canvas carrier emblazoned with her name that hangs from Miss Savannah's shoulder. I am toted by the female trainer, Casey, in a hand-held plastic carrier that scrapes the floor now and then.

"Man, this is a big old boy," the trainer complains, loping along behind the click of Miss Savannah's high heels.

"My little Yvette," Miss Savannah Ashleigh answers with smug possession, "is as light as a marabou feather." Even I can hear my human travel companion grit her teeth (which are lamentably dull to begin with). Soon, however, I am slung to the cushy leather of a first-class seat. Too bad this plastic shell is between me and it. In the next moment I am thumped onto the airplane carpeting and shoved under the seat ahead, where it is dark and the floorboards thrum like a generator. Forget first class when you are feline and no purebred, so I tune out until I can cut to the chase. In this case, the commercial shoot is slated for a state of the union called Massachusetts. 🐾

Chapter 2

Glamour Puss

Filming Cat Food commercials may sound glamourous, but I find it to be work. Especially "location" shoots. Once I am delivered to the "set," in short order I find myself afloat on choppy seas, attired in a yellow oilcloth slicker and rain hat to the point of anonymity, being swept toward the Divine Yvette (who is more the Supine Yvette at the moment) by giant fans.

The Divine Yvette is clinging to a red buoy tooth and nail, her aquamarine eyes wide with a fright more manic than cinematic.

I am an old hand at the bounding Main, however, having mastered a dunking in the Treasure Island hotel's pirate-ship cove during one of my cases. And my old man did time on a tuna trawler in the Pacific northwest, so the sea is in my veins.

This body of waves, however, is not even a first cousin to the sea. We two are but adrift on the fan-blown surface of an aboveground swimming pool, circled by a whole crew of potential rescuers, if guys toting expensive video cameras and high-voltage cables can be trusted to leap into the water on missions of mercy for four-footed friends they do not know from Rin Tin Tin.

In fact, the camera crew, hired locally—i.e., Ben and Jerry out of New York City—is hip, downright serious, and carries far more equipment than one would need to capture two emoting kitty cats for an À La Cat commercial. Perhaps they are from the method school of feline filming.

The scent of saltwater sensors the brisk autumn air, though, for our portable pond is set up on the rocky shingle along the Atlantic ocean. Beyond us the big waves roll in like green anchovy Jell-O, unbroken for thousands of miles except by a low black scowl of rock that looks like a beached sting ray, name of Devil Reef, they say.

My vessel is only a miniature plywood trawler, not the beautiful pea-green boat famed in poesy for romantically inclined pussycats. (And what is so beautiful about pea-green, I ask? Especially since it is the color of a pasty-faced human with mal de mer.) If you want a beautiful nautical color, you will find it in the sea-green eyes of the Divine Yvette, even when she is more than somewhat seasick, as she is at the moment.

"Louie," she wails piteously. "Get me out of here. *Now!*"

What can I do? I am only an actor adrift in my part. But I gallantly throw my weight forward to hasten my arrival at her side. This nearly capsizes my unseaworthy cork, so I bound onto the nearing buoy, which lurches wildly in the waves.

"Cut! Cut!" The director screams from the dry, stable distance.

Water, cold and distinctly wet, laps my darling's curled and clawed little toes. My own tail is as soggy as a salt-drenched cable. Finally, the big fans buzz to a dead stop, the waves wane, and Casey wades into the knee-deep water to retrieve us.

"It is a wrap," the director yells.

And wrap it is. The Divine One is soon encompassed by a pink velour bath towel and subsequently cradled in her crooning mistress's arms. I am wrapped in a skimpy brown terrycloth hand towel and crammed dripping into my carrier.

Then we are both whisked back to the Gilman House Bed

and Breakfast. If I wanted a change of pace from Las Vegas, I have got it in spades. This burg is so backward it does not even have a McDonald's. I mean, who has ever heard of a half-abandoned coastal Massachusetts fishing town called Innsmouth?

But I understand that we are here because for some reason the fish flock to this literal backwater, and the area has plenty of local color in the form of fishing boats, buoys and such.

Now that I am out of the south-Easter outfit and ensconced in the dingy bedroom assigned to Casey, I think about what to do for entertainment on an Innsmouth Friday night. This is always a prime fish-eating day of the week in some circles, and in my circles any day is scale day for me. I have not spotted any carp ponds, but the entire bay is teeming with finned creatures, I am given to understand, so I hanker to do a little cruising.

I love bed and breakfast places. It is so easy to get in and out of rooms there, what with no chain locks, etcetera. The only television is in the parlor, and there I find Miss Savannah Ashleigh in a turquoise Spandex gym outfit so tight and shiny you would think she was a cellophane-wrapped sausage with a bad case of mold.

She is watching some funky old horror film on the black-and-white television set (I kid you not!), and giggling with the director, Mr. Mitch Marshall, who wears only one earring with his designer jeans and Izod shirts and is the only eligible male (of her species) around.

Sure enough, beside her chair slumps the Divine Yvette's carrier—empty.

I look around and spot my lovely reclining against the wall as far away from the television set as she can manage. Apparently her mistress is viewing one of her old movies.

"Oh, God!" Miss Savannah Ashleigh says. "I cannot believe I was ever desperate enough to make this Reggie Borman film. It

7

was supposed to be set right around here, but of course we filmed it in California. Look at me! I am wearing *bell-bottoms!*"

"I cannot believe you are old enough to have ever worn bell-bottoms," Mr. Mitch Marshall says with the insincere tone of guys in bars trying to manage a pickup.

I ankle over to the wall to pitch some woo of my own.

"Hello there, Beautiful, I see that you are out of your customary container."

"My mistress took me out for a lap session, but then that lying Lothario came along and she forgot all about me. I am not accustomed to being forgotten," she says with a head toss that sets her silver ruff in sensual motion, like a wave of warm, soft velour.

"Then let us escape this dull joint for a night on the town."

"I am not allowed out alone at night, or any time else."

"That is as it should be for a delicate little doll like you, but you did not have a suitable escort before who was big and brawny enough to protect you from every eventuality."

The Divine Yvette still looks adorably doubtful, so I jerk my head to her delinquent mistress, who is even now accepting a refill in her glass from a large jug of liquorous nature.

"I am so glad you brought your own," Miss Savannah Ashleigh is cooing to Mr. Marshall. "This town does not have a liquor store or even a Starbuck's, can you imagine?"

"I can imagine that we will be a lot cosier here tonight," he whispers back. "The loco yokels advised the crew that they have some special Halloween ceremony tonight and we should stay off the streets. A religious observance, I guess."

"Hey, they do not have to encourage me to stay off these nasty, narrow, nauseatingly smelly streets! Why on earth did we end up filming here?"

Mr. Mitch Marshall shrugs. "Lots of fish. For some reason everything has dried up in Innsmouth but the fish and the boats.

And with the town so decrepit, there was no city council to demand film permits and paperwork. We can come in and do what we want."

"Oooh, but the place is so creepy." Miss Savannah Ashleigh shivers most unconvincingly, but Mr. Mitch Marshall falls for the act enough to put his arm around her twitching shoulders. "It is much scarier than that old Reggie Borman film, which I guess was based on some weird stories by a writer who used to live in the region."

"Worry not," Mr. Mitch Marshall says, "we will hide away here and have our own trick or treat party."

They are silent for a while, pursuing courtship rituals that I always try to avoid seeing. Humans are so disgusting. I can tell that the Divine Yvette agrees, for she has turned her face to the wall.

"Ready for a holiday getaway?" I ask.

"How can I? My mistress will notice that my carrier is empty eventually."

"Not if I can help it."

She lilts the airy whiskers above her eyes and watches with rounded pupils when I slink over to the carrier. I spot some sort of lumpish neck pillow on the floor and drag it to the carrier. In two minutes I have stuffed the pillow into the carrier and drawn the zipper shut, using my saber-tooth as an implement.

I am back at the Divine Yvette's shaded silver side before she can whistle "cockles and mussels, alive, alive-o."

"Oh, Louie, you are so clever. But what will we do in this Bast-forsaken town if it is as dismal as my mistress and her . . . companion say?"

"Hey, I bet I can find some hot spots a pair of hep cats like us would groove on, and, besides, your mistress is laboring under a big handicap. Humans do not *like* the smell of fish, especially lots and lots of fish. I can get you some fresh catch wholesale."

All the while I am talking I am nudging the Divine Yvette onto her pretty pale little paws and along the wall to the door. It is a rather dingy, dusty wall, so I try to keep her elegant coat from brushing against it. I am nothing if not a gentleman.

We are through the door without anyone's notice. I had seen before that the other crew members had retired to their rooms with whatever private stock they had. For some reason the entire party has been acting a bit depressed ever since we hit town.

But I am exuberant. Here we are, my baby and me, about to step out on our own to paint the town red. It is our first dinner date, and I intend to make it one that the Divine Yvette will never forget.

Chapter 3

Legend-Shadowed Innsmouth

We INHALE the marvelous aroma of the brisk sea air, part cod and halibut, part lobster, part something indescribable.

The Divine Yvette's little rose nose wrinkles. "I must agree with my mistress. Since I have been eating Free-to-be-Feline I have become something of a vegetarian. The odor in the streets certainly is rather . . . fishy."

"'Fishy' is perfume to the feline nation. I am sure that with all these scaled beauties about, our kind patronizes many tasty hideaways down by the waterline. What do you say to a lobster dinner tonight?"

"I do not eat anything I have to remove from a natural casing. I could break a nail."

"I will de-shell the lobster for you, so you have only to nibble on the delicious white meat."

"Oh, very well."

We amble shoulder to shoulder down a dark narrow street. High shuttered houses on both sides hide the stars, and even the moon, but I know that a full one beckons tonight. I can feel its pull in the saltwater within my veins. This will be a momentous evening for Yvette and myself, romantic beyond my imaginings of this moment, which are many and not fit for family consumption.

As I think of consumption, my stomach growls.

"What was that?" The Divine Yvette is cowering in a shadow.

"Nothing, my dear." I improvise quickly. "Probably trick or treaters prowling in their mock-monster costumes, making noises to match. We know what real growls are."

She nods, and resumes walking. We are not making tracks for any world speed records. The Divine Yvette walks like Marilyn Monroe, tiny baby steps, each foot crossing in front of the other. It gives her lush tail a delightful rhumba motion that must be seen to be appreciated.

I am lagging behind to enjoy the view when she jumps back from an intersection, her fur coat fluffed up like a silvered tumbleweed.

"What is it, my pet?" I inquire in a tone of studly confidence.

"Something . . . someone is down that street."

I peer carefully around the corner, keeping my eyes almost slitted shut so they do not reflect the light and draw any undue attention.

This time the Divine Yvette's exquisite nerves are not imagining anything. Shambling figures are indeed doing the hokey pokey down the avenue, such as it is. A fresh wave of fish perfume almost makes *me* swoon, but I cling to consciousness and view their oddly chinless profiles. Some hidden beam of moonlight reflects off their silvered eyes . . . fixed and inexpressive. Their feet barely leave the ground when they walk and they make a scaly, scraping noise as they move that quite intrigues me. My stomach tries to growl again, but I exert all my self-control to quash it. I cannot embarrass the Divine Yvette on our first dinner date by showing too rampant an appetite.

As I am so occupied battling my worse self, a new figure comes into view, one that hops! Yet it is human size. Perhaps all

13

these trick or treaters are masquerading as Frankenstein's monster, or at least their impression of him. These Innsmouth types are a backward, isolated, inbred lot, from what I have heard.

None of this disturbs me, however; certain feral clans of my kind have been forced into a dab of inbreeding, with no untoward results, other than the usual deplorable population explosion.

There is no population explosion in Innsmouth. From all I have heard, the town has been decimated for decades, and yet so many of these sober Halloween celebrators pass, an entire procession, all of them slobbering and glubbing and squeaking every now and then. And they all seem to be adults, no wee ones out at all.

Despite the heavenly piscine odor, I am touched by a bit of the Divine Yvette's diffidence.

"Let us head for the seaside," I tell her. "I doubt that these trick or treaters will be out long, though; few houses looked occupied."

"But there are faint lights in the upper stories of some of these ruins," she points out with a well-manicured mitt. "And I have seen strange, humped shadows shuffling past the drawn shades."

"Having a Halloween party, no doubt. Probably dunking for apples. Now, down this alleyway and a few blocks further, and we will be near enough to dip our toes in the tide."

"I do not like water," the Divine Yvette observes in a tone that some might call prissy. Or even pouty. "And my footpads are beginning to hurt from the hard, damp, cold cobblestones."

"Only a street or two more, and I swear the mighty sea itself shall be lapping at our feet as if we were the King and Queen of Tides."

I am relieved to see no more shambling figures as we break onto the shoreline, only a few tented fishing nets, the moonlight visible at last, painting the waves with silver streaks so the ocean looks like a great, purring shaded silver Persian cat, asleep in the deep.

I inhale happily. "Ah, nothing like the sea air to enhance

an appetite. Is not the moonlight romantic?" I then compare the gently heaving sea to the great, purring shaded silver Persian cat, etcetera.

The Divine Yvette rewards my poetic soul with a coquettish rub against my polished black satin dinner jacket. "What a lovely sentiment, Louie. I should know that you are called 'Midnight' because the night-time brings out the best in you."

Hey, who needs dinner? By now the exciting fish smell has become as old hat as Sinatra's second-favorite fedora. I can inhale only the heady aroma of pheromones of the feline persuasion, and dare to nuzzle the Divine muzzle.

I am not rebuffed.

This could be my lucky Halloween.

We are dancing cheek to cheek in the moonlight and I think I am in cat heaven, when suddenly the Divine Yvette freezes stiff as a mummy.

I follow the glassy gaze of her aquamarine eyes. She is staring out toward Devil Reef with the concentration of a predator born.

This reaction is unexpected in one who has led such an unnaturally sheltered life. There is not much prey to stare at on Rodeo Drive, unless it is a pink poodle the size of a guinea pig.

"Louie," she breathes in a tone of barely controlled excitement.

My pulses race.

"If the sea is this beautiful, panting, shaded silver Persian whose exquisite coat ripples in the night air, I have news for you."

"Yes, my love?"

"This Persian has *fleas!*"

She sounds most insulted, even peeved, so I gaze more carefully at the gentle moonlit swells between us and the distant Devil Reef.

The waves are a-swarm with small dark specks, all moving to land.

"Could it be . . . grunion?" I wonder.

"Grunion?"

"Schools of spawn-happy fish who beach themselves at night. But these fishy full-moon freaks are native to the California coast, naturally . . ."

We hunker behind a fish-net curtain to watch. As the spots near land, they enlarge, and then they come lumbering out of the water, upright (if you can quite call it that). I am reminded of zombies, of generations of sunken sailors called up from the Deep.

Some are robed, others bare and shiny, almost . . . slimy.

The fishy odor gathers into a tidal wave and washes over us with these creatures' passage. It is almost unbearable, even to the feline nose. Yvette buries her little face in my side, trembling with distaste.

I watch the parade pass, scraping and hopping, in an almost human gait, yet quite . . . animal. No, not animal and not quite reptilian, though there is something cold-blooded about the moonlit horde humping and jumping ashore. Perhaps ichythoid is the word, a way of saying "fishy" in a more scientific vein.

Now slobbers and croaks come from the passing throng.

We watch until the last ambiguous figure has slithered inland.

"Not lobster," I mutter.

"What did you say, Louie?" comes Yvette's smothered voice.

"Nothing important, my love. I merely said I think we could dine in the French fashion tonight. On frog legs. Lots of very large frog legs . . ."

 Chapter 4

Shuddered Windows

BY NOW EVEN a love-blinded Weimaraner would know that something sinister is afoot (or ahop). I tell the Divine Yvette that I will escort her back to the bed and breakfast before leaving on a solo investigation. Dinner will have to wait.

She clings to me like a lissome furred leech. "Do not leave me, Louie! If you do, we will never meet again, I know."

"Do not be silly. I investigate fishy doings all the time, and there is a lot more larceny, felony and homicide abroad in Vegas than ever could occur in a puddle in the road like Innsmouth."

So we make our silent, stealthy way back to the byway that hosts the Gilman House. It is not easy. The streets teem with ranks of rank-smelling Halloween revelers, and by now the fishy smell has become a stench redolent of decay. Occasionally a more human figure moves among the loping, snuffling minions, and that sight chills me more than I can say. If anything human lives in this cursed town, it is in service to the misbegotten, mutated multitudes that rule the streets tonight.

We pass an intersection that leads to a square only two blocks away, when I spot an apparent church building, its high thin windows lit by eerie, underwater motes. I glimpse a figure in a trailing robe wearing some sort of Miss America crown, only this tiara gleams with unearthly, unwholesome colors.

Then, amidst the surrounding inarticulate mutters so like a washing seashore, a human voice speaks.

"What about the visitors?"

I stop so suddenly that the Divine Yvette is pressed between me and the wall like a feather duster.

"They are all . . . at the G-g-gilman House." This second voice has thickened beyond the human, and breaks into high-pitched croaks like a teenage boy on every other syllable.

The lights from the square cast distorted shadows on the wall opposite us. I will say this for the Divine Yvette: sheltered she may be and scared out of her stripes, but she does not make a peep during this eavesdropping interlude.

"We will come for them later. No outsiders can escape during our semiannual celebration. They might see something to speak of after they leave."

"They will not . . . *glug* . . . leave."

The speakers are swallowed by the shuffle and hop of many feet, all pouring into the church building as if it were a bottomless pit.

"Come on," I tell my darling. "You must get back to the bed and breakfast."

"But you heard! Even that is not safe. My poor mistress! And she is wearing only her second-best work-out ensemble. She would die if she were to perish in such a state!"

"No one will perish. I am on the case. I am going to get to the bottom of what is happening here, and then I will stop it."

"One, against hundreds?"

"You heard them. They can barely speak, much less think."

"But what will you do?"

"I will infiltrate their ranks to discover who they really are

18

and what this is all about. And then I will think of something."

By now we are back at the shabby door to the bed and breakfast. I see that high in the attic a faint light now gleams, but I do not mention this to the Divine Yvette.

"Louie, you are so brave. I cannot let you risk yourself. We will raise an alarm within and—"

"And what?"

"Well, I will yowl like a banshee, then shiver and stand all my hairs on end as if I have had the world's worse permanent wave. My mistress will know that something terrible is happening and insist that I get instant veterinary care and that we all leave immediately."

"You may and she may, but will anyone else rouse themselves in the middle of the night because you might be having a bad hair day? This not the Hollywood Hills, my girl, this is Nowheresville. People have never listened to our kind before. In fact, in this very neck of the woods, a few hundred years ago, during the witch hunts on this very night, they put plenty of our forebears to the torch too."

"No!"

"Yes! And did you notice something odd about this town?"

"Everything?"

"Besides that. Did you spot anything on four legs beyond the usual wharf rats? Any cats? Any dogs?"

"You think they were all—"

"I think they know better than to hang around Innsmouth, especially on Halloween."

"And especially one of your color, Louie! You must go back. I will investigate. I am not the suspect color, I will—"

"—stand out like a silver Mercedes-Benz in a parking lot full of green Volkswagens." The Divine Yvette lowers her lashes. "Thank you, Louie. I know you meant that comparison well, but

I really consider myself more of the Ferrari type, possibly a Testa Rossa."

"Whatever wheels you think you are, baby, they are chrome-plated wire ones. Now go back in like a good girl, and try to calm everyone down."

"It will be hard," she sniffles, "but I will use my most soporific purr. I will even rub against that miserable so-called animal trainer who kept my Free-to-be-Feline away for six hours so I would perform for a bit of nasty, slimy, smelly raw sardine!"

"There is a brave girl."

I paw open a broken-down front window and give the Divine Yvette a lift up via a slightly sharp farewell pat on the rump. What a world-class tail!

Then I am off on errands of a peculiarly repellent nature.

Who would think that it would ever be Midnight Louie vs. the fish-folk? All my street days spearing carp from decorative ponds have not been for naught. Although my night-black coat was trouble for my kind in the old days, it does allow me to merge with the dark. I dart from shadow to shadow as I near the square that houses the church.

A religious ceremony, the director had been told, was being held tonight. But what religion? With so many frog-folk present, I might suspect a Roman Catholic bent, but there is nothing remotely French in this town except for the Divine Yvette, and she only has periodic pretensions to being French, having been born and bred in Burbank, California.

I spy the graven letters on another building in the square: "Esoteric Order of Dagon." (At first I take it for Order of Dragon, but apparently these debased types in Innsmouth do not know how to spell, because there is no "r" in the word. Actually, sometimes my own spelling is a trifle shaky so I am not one to point a paw at others' deficiencies.)

The joint that is jumping is one of the two churches facing the square, a queer edifice with a high, above-ground basement and shuttered windows.

Getting in on the ground floor will be easier, I figure, and besides, someone left the door open. I boogie in as quietly as a church mouse . . . which they also do not seem to have in this town. Above me I hear the thump and jump and slobber and glub and inhuman croaking of the worshipers.

I have heard and seen a lot of untoward revelry in Las Vegas in my time, but nothing that compares to what I can only imagine is going on above.

The fish odor is particularly fetid down here, where the stone and dirt floor is not only damp, but slimy, as if six thousand snails had done the bunny hop all over the place.

Nobody or nothing appears to be in residence now, dancing or not. I mince carefully forward to keep from slipping on the slime and bump right into an altar. Above it, hangs an oil lamp that sways as if we were at sea, but is just reacting to the uproar above.

Around the stone block are carved strange, coiling creatures and letters formed into words of no language known on earth, and I have seen Sanskrit, Cyrilliac, Arabic, and plain old Yak on my travels among the deacquisitioned library books.

Iä-R'eallyeah! Cthulhu phhhht again! Iä! Iä! I can assure one and all that this is *not* Greek to me. Since the language is so unreadable I concentrate on the pictographs. My kind was worshiped in ancient Egypt, so we have a hereditary gift for glyphs.

To study the frieze of strange figures, which runs just below the top of the altar, I will have to leap on top of it. Ugh! I gather myself and spring into the oily darkness until the faint lamplight warms my back.

I crouch atop a stone surface sticky with green ichor, as if those conga-line snails had given up the ghost here. Above me the cacophony reaches an unholy pitch. The entire building shakes with the sound and fury, until the shutters rattle on their hinges.

At any moment I expect my sanctuary to be violated by the humped celebrants, but I crane my neck over the edge and endeavor to interpret the figures upside down. Actually, they look more attractive that way. I follow the frieze around, spying an island in an immense ocean, with a tribe of humans on bended knee to something that rises from the sea.

Another scene shows a sailing ship amid ruffled waves . . . with something as huge and humped as Devil Reef following behind as if towed. The next glyph depicts flying fish leaping from the waves before a shoreline remarkably like that edging Innsmouth, and a long, low ridge of reef at the rim of the deeper depths.

It is while I am making my sticky circuit of the frieze that my second-most-sensitive rear member makes a bit of unexpected contact with something. I freeze myself, wondering what shares the altar-top with me. Then I turn, back and tail humped, hair electrified. In the swaying lantern light, I spot a small stone statue, a carving of alien design, showing something so huge and degraded, a mix of sub-aquatic mystery . . . of giant squid and mismated octopus, of shark and serpent and still something that speaks of a human face on the shapeless sac of a head . . . It is as if I am seeing the rotted remains of all hidden bloated beasts of the Deeps, reanimated into a revolting new being, into a god so debased that it would give the Devil a good name. Dagon? Or this Cthulhu character?

Whoever, its presence here, and that of its myriad of worshipers above, does not bode well for the bodily and mental safety of the À La Cat commercial film crew.

Leaping from the altar-top down to the slimy floor, I bolt into the dark until I find a rickety wooden stairway to the upper regions. Now I can hear faintly human voices chanting, and I run for that last vestige of sanity.

I burst into the upper church unseen, soon lost in a forest of swaying garments, moisture-darkened along their hems. Croaking, guttural syllables surround me. I weave, overcome by a lethal concentration of fish odor, like cod-liver oil force-fed to a newborn litter. I brush against the revolting vestments and the even more revolting wearers underneath.

And then I smell something else. Expensive leather.

These Innsmouth throwbacks fancy . . . Fendi? Gucci? *Iä! Iä! Versace?* Give me a break! Innsmouth is the antithesis of Rodeo Drive. So I dive under an ichor-soaked robe hem (ick, indeed!), following the scent of designer lambskin, and run right into a black leather backpack. Interesting. Next to it stand the limbs of the creature within. The light leaks through the robe's loose weave, so I unsquinch my eyes and prepare to view the feet I had heard sucking and slurping and slopping and hopping along the Innsmouth byways all night. I expect size-twelve tentacles by now.

I see size ten Reeboks.

I am not alone.

It takes but a couple minutes of listening and looking to figure out the situation. I am not the only escapee from the Gilman House Bed and Breakfast this Halloween night. Ben and Jerry are out on the town too, in native disguise. So are their cameras, concealed inside the leather bags underneath their disgusting robes. Beneath the raucous uproar, I hear the subtle whirr of hidden tapes recording the goings-on.

Well, well, well. Hello, *Sixty Minutes.*

However, knowing that you are not alone on the Titanic may be only momentarily comforting, like singing "Nearer, My God, to Thee."

I do not fancy meeting the cat-god Bastet with snail-ichor on my tootsies. And I most particularly do not fancy encountering the local deity with the suction-cup manicure and the Bette Davis eyes.

But this cannot be helped. Even if someone human is here recording the distinctly inhuman doings, only the Head Guy can stop the forthcoming carnage. I must go to the top.

Chapter 5

The Thing From the Deeps

So I RETRACE my sticky steps back to the basement, then out the door to the empty streets. I must return to the site of my romantic interlude with the Divine Yvette, but romance is not on my mind.

Unnoticed by any but those who claw like rats at the shuttered windows of the attics as I pass by, I streak through the streets of Innsmouth as if pursued by demons, or Dagons.

My route takes me past the bed and breakfast, where I am nearly tripped by an extraordinarily luxurious tail that is thrust into my path.

I right myself, sputtering.

The Divine Yvette is posed on the worn stoop, looking adorably determined.

"There are strange creaking and croaking sounds on the floor above our rooms, Louie. I will not be able to get a wink of sleep tonight, anyway. And our valiant cameramen, Ben and Jerry, are missing. I am going with you. Do not try to stop me."

"You have no idea of what I must waken. You have not seen the graven stones, the writhing, rotting heart of Evil grown bloated with the death-swollen carnage of endless eons and bottomless depths. You have not heard the sobbing, gibbering cries of its victims, its worshipers who crawl and hop, croak and creep to lick the pustules of its undulating feet. The horror, the horror!"

My sincerity gives her pause. She shakes her ruff into apple-pie order. "But I have seen, and heard, my mistress when she first glimpses her unmade-up face in the mirror in the morning. I believe I can confront anything. I call upon Bast to protect us."

I want to argue that even the ancient Egyptian cat goddess Bastet is a pretty puny force to invoke against the likes of this Cthulhu-dude; besides, I did not know that the Divine Yvette had a religious streak.

"Should we not hurry?" she demands.

I cannot argue with that, so I take off again, surprised to find the flying fur of the Divine Yvette at my shoulder. When this babe said she had Ferrari ambitions she was not kidding.

We twist and turn through the deserted, damp byways, nearing the seashore and the fetid tide that washed a wave of

aquatic flotsam from Hell upon this forgotten Innsmouth shore for Halloween night.

Behind me I hear a soft pattering, like rain. But nothing falls from the sky, or wets my tongue when I stick it out. The sound multiplies until it is like a clap of hands at a magician's show. I twist my head, envisioning a Pied Piper's-worth of rats, the only creatures I can feature sharing this shuddersome town with its loathsome inhabitants.

A mob of racing feet and wind-whipped tails does indeed pursue us: dark hunched forms with pale incisors gleaming.

I lengthen my stride. The Divine Yvette matches me, her pink tongue unrolling with effort. We rush onto the beach and into the moonlight, where I turn back to gauge our pursuers' closeness.

Soon we will be rat-meat.

But these are exceptionally large rats. As I look I see that all

of them are black like me, and some seem . . . charred, and some heads loll at impossible angles. There are dozens and dozens of them, eerily silent, pouring out of the streets of Innsmouth—a legion of black cats, Halloween cats, witches' cats, hunted and hung and burned by the thousands and millions hundreds of years ago. They are massing behind us like a many-headed, footed, tailed monster, coming to confront something like the embodiment of the ancient evil mania that killed them.

"Do not look back," I caution the Divine Yvette so strictly that she actually obeys me. "Our enemy is before us, on that forsaken stretch of rock they call Devil Reef."

Then, facing the sea empty of all apparent living things, including fish, I intone the words I saw spelled out on the basement altar.

There is silence under the moon, and behind us only the soft, rapid sound of ghost cats panting. The dead do not breathe, and the beast does not come when called. Even if a cat may look at a queen, a cat may not summon a monster.

Yet an ancient antagonism exists between catkind and the denizens of deep water, and in the pallid moonlit I finally see Devil Reef rise, as if the rocks were being driven upward by a tremendous force, an underwater volcano of vengeance and venom.

What hath Bast and Midnight Louie wrought?

The entire dark reef seems to swell, floating, bloating to meet us. Like an oil slick, the shadow darkens the moon-streaked waves, assembling into the bat-black form of a manta ray as large as the dark side of the moon.

Greasy black waves crash over the breakwater stones. They lick their way up the sand, liquid velvet spawned in Hell.

I would retreat but am mindful of the black mass of feline ghouls behind us. Talk about being caught between the Devil and the deep black sea! My only regret is that the Divine Yvette's fate is signed, sealed and delivered. Nothing will be left of us but an errant whisker by the time this deep-sea leviathan is done.

The body of the beast stretches now from the shore to the reef, as if evil were elastic. It begins to rear up, an amorphous mountain. I see tangled tentacles like the exposed roots of swamp cypress trees. A corpulent, boneless body spreads like pus and a great scaly head looms: a wild, half-human expression in its twenty-feet-high eyes; flat, silver eyes with bottomless holes of black pin-pricks at the soul-less center. . . .

Yet there comes another rising. Behind us. The hissing is at first surf-like, then it becomes a more sinister sound, resembling a hellish fire roaring out of control. I look back, as I urged the Divine Yvette not to do.

The cats . . . the dead cats have risen into a mountain of hissing, spitting forms, black outlined by spectral flames that shoot from gleaming eyes and snarl-shaped mouths.

I blink and look back to the beast from below. It is reaching a height to obscure the moon. Tentacles lash in the ebony ooze of the beach. A whip of suction cups rises above me, then curls around my midsection.

It is like being crushed by an electric eel. I lift off the ground, flailing my feet, my fabled shivs slashing only air.

"Stop that!" the Divine Yvette snarls, "you nasty, scaly, slimy, raw, fishy thing. *Iäääää!*"

Her martial-arts howl would wake the dead, had Bast not done so already. Pale, exquisitely sharpened claws curve into scimitars in the moonlit. Churning limbs attack the tentacle like a buzz-saw.

I feel a sudden sag at my middle and plummet to sand.

Behind us the cat chorus has reached a pitch that could drown out the clamor of Cthulhu's worshipers, and apparently has.

The black shape on the water shrinks, withdraws, becomes

one again with Devil Reef. At last the sea is still, and so is the night.

I look behind again. All that masses there is a pile of charred deadwood.

Then I eye the Divine Yvette, whose unkempt ruff is a spiky silver halo. She looks more than a little like a punk rocker.

Her expression is one of unutterable disgust, but it is not directed at me, I am relieved to say. Instead she is staring toward the sand at our feet.

"Hey!" Things are definitely looking up. "You snared a prime hunk of calamari there. An unusual color. Maybe we should call it 'blackened calamari.' Looks like we can have that seafood dinner for two, after all."

Her disgusted look turns in my direction.

"I do not eat sushi," she says. "And who knows where this stuff has been?"

Chapter 6

Escape from Innsmouth

WELL, IT IS ALL OVER, including the shouting.

By the time the Divine Yvette and I return to the bed and breakfast, Ben and Jerry are back, the van that brought us here is now parked out front. They are loading the others and their equipment, and urging all possible speed.

Our arrival is greeted with shrieks of relief. We are, after all, the stars of this little epicurean epic. Despite our status, we are tossed unceremoniously into the back of the van, sans carriers.

This allows me to cosy up to the Divine Yvette, who sits washing and washing her feet as if the scent of seafood will never come off.

"I would have liked to have kept it as a souvenir, at least," I say, regretting the hunk of Cthulhu left languishing on the beach for the tide to take.

"I suppose you would have had it mounted. Dirty, smelly old dead thing. Males!"

"How did you manage to do so much damage with those dainty little nails of yours?"

"For one thing, they have never been worn down by common activities like street-walking. And my secret for their luxurious length and strength is in the special variety of scratching post I use."

"Oh? I have always found an old fence sufficient."

"Please. I work out indoors, and only on Mommy's best, stretchiest Spandex leotards. This is what also buffs the surface for a special sheen."

She fans the shivs on her right mitt in demonstration while I nod.

The ride back to Boston is exceedingly fast and bumpy. En route, we drowse while Ben and Jerry explain to the others what they think has happened. I listen, trying not to smirk.

"We had an extra, undercover assignment all along," Ben says. "See, we are independent reporters, and word has it that Innsmouth has suffered for decades from unreported, unaddressed toxic waste. That whole bay out there is a pool of putrefaction from the Marsh family refinery."

"Oh," Miss Savannah Ashleigh croons in concern. "Yvette and I drank the water!"

"What we had was well water," Ben assures her. "The remaining residents are not completely unaware of their degraded environment. But did you notice their wan, unhealthy look?

"They all looked pale, and scaly and chinless. What they need around here is a good plastic surgeon."

"No," says Jerry firmly. "They need to have the whole bay cleaned up by the EPA. You are right that the 'Innsmouth look' is unhealthy. The skin disease, poor posture, and bone damage are caused by eating tainted fish products. The town was so isolated—and after the pollution got a grip on the place, the neighbors became superstitiously afraid of the poor souls—that no one in authority was aware of how bad things had become.

"By then the victims had suffered brain damage and made their own decline into a religious cult. It is amazing what isolation and ignorance will do, even in this enlightened age. This is a bigger story than Love Canal, and we have lots of footage for the evening news. Believe me, once this piece runs, the government will be in here cleaning up their act like gangbusters. Our undercover jaunt will put an end to it all."

"My poor baby!" Miss Savannah Ashleigh pouts, turning in her seat to look at us. "She was lured outdoors by that awful alley cat. I hope she was not exposed to anything toxic."

"No chance. All the action tonight was in that bizarre church."

I beg to differ, but am too polite to say so.

They would be Cthulhu meat, every last one of them, had not I determined the root cause of the commotion and decided to broach the demon on his very own turf and surf.

And, I admit to myself, I would be Cthulhu-meat myself, had not the Divine Yvette called on Bast for literal back-up and used her awesome shivs on the great big bully from Beyond.

So it was Beauty vs. the Beast, but the beast-limb at least would have been Louie-meat if not for the Divine Yvette's delicate sensibilities.

At least I can tell my old man about the Great Old One that got away. 🐾

H. P. LOVECRAFT (1890-1937) was the premier horror writer of his time, and continues to exert an influence on practitioners of that dark art. Most of his work is unified by a common theme—the Cthulhu (kuh-tool-ew) Mythos—in which gods furtively control the fate of mortals, and a mere glimpse of the universe, by nature hostile, is enough to drive a man insane. A number of Lovecraft's peers borrowed the Mythos for use in their own stories, launching a tradition that contuinues in our day.

Publishers Weekly

Tales of the Cthulhu Mythos by H. P. Lovecraft

The Nameless City *1921*
The Call of Cthulhu *1922*
The Case of Charles Dexter Ward *1926*
The Color Out of Space *1927*
The Dunwich Horror *1928*
The Haunter of the Dark *1929*
The Whisperer in Darkness *1930*
At the Mountains of Madness *1931*
The Shadow Over Innsmouth *1931*
The Dreams in the Witch-House *1932*
The Thing on the Doorstep *1933*
The Shadow Out of Time *1934*

Also by Carole Nelson Douglas

The Midnight Louie mystery series

Catnap ... Pussyfoot
Cat on a Blue Monday • Cat in a Crimson Haze
Cat in a Diamond Dazzle • Cat with an Emerald Eye
Cat in a Flamingo Fedora • Cat in a Golden Garland
Cat on a Hyacinth Hunt • Cat in an Indigo Mood
Cat in a Jeweled Jumpsuit • Cat in a Kiwi Con
Cat in a Leopard Spot • Cat in a Midnight Choir
Cat in a Neon Nightmare • Cat in an Orange Twist

Short Story Anthologies:

Midnight Louie's Pet Detectives
White House Pet Detectives

The Midnight Louie Romantic Suspense Quartet

Crystal Days (two novels per volume, 1990)
Crystal Nights (two novels per volume, 1990)
Revised and reissued in 1999–2000 as:
The Cat and the King of Clubs
The Cat and the Queen of Hearts
The Cat and the Jill of Diamonds
The Cat and the Jack of Spades

The Irene Adler Sherlockian Suspense Novels

Good Night, Mr. Holmes
The Adventuress (formerly Good Morning, Irene)
A Soul of Steel (formerly Irene at Large)
Another Scandal in Bohemia (formerly Irene's Last Waltz)
Chapel Noir
Castle Rouge
Femme Fatale
Spider Dance (Sept 2004)

Mystery's benign Godfather

Ed Gorman

Ed Gorman became a full-time writer after spending twenty years in advertising, mostly writing and directing TV commercials in Chicago and the Midwest. While Ed is generally regarded as a crime novelist, he has also written a number of westerns and horror novels, and he reads voraciously in all genres. Several of his books and stories have been optioned for film. He is the founder and, until recently, was the editor of *Mystery Scene* magazine. A prolific novelist and editor, his projects under both hats number over a hundred. Ed Gorman currently writes the Sam McCain series of nostalgic mysteries set in the 1950s and 1960s. *Kirkus Reviews* calls him "one of the most original suspense writers around."As editor of the long-running "Cat Crimes" series of mystery anthologies, Ed solicited and bought Carole Nelson Douglas's first published short story, a Midnight Louie *Maltese Falcon* pastiche titled "The Maltese Double Cross." Carole considers Ed the benign "Godfather" of the mystery field for his important role in encouraging writers of all genres and both genders. He lives in Cedar Rapids, Iowa, with his wife, novelist Carol Gorman, and their three cats.

Brad W. Foster with his "mews" Sable
Photo by Cindy Guyton

BRAD W. FOSTER

ILLUSTRATOR, cartoonist, writer, and publisher of Jabberwocky Graphix of Irving, Texas, Brad W. Foster's illustrations have appeared in 2,000 publications, half of them science fiction fanzines. His intricate pen and ink work has also graced such genre magazines as *Amazing Stories* and *Dragon*. He's won the science fiction field's Hugo Award for best fan artist five times, as well as a Chelsea award. He created his own comic series, The Mechthings, and for a few years was the official "Big Background Artist" for Image Comic's *Shadowhawk*. His work has also appeared in such mainstream magazines as *Cat Fancy, Cavalier,* and *Highlights for Children*. Brad's most recent work includes Yard Dog Press book covers and illustrations for *Space & Time* and *Talebones* magazines. He even managed to work a dragon into the official poster for the 2003 Tulsa Oktoberfest. Brad, his wife Cindy, and their four cats, Sable, Duffy, Tiger, and Vlad, share a fifties-vintage Dallas house that includes a huge two-story studio full of marvels and monsters.

bwfoster@juno.com

About the Author

Carole Nelson Douglas's forty-some published novels include mystery and suspense, science fiction, high fantasy, women's mainstream and romance titles. The first woman to write female-focused Sherlockiana, she reinvented Irene Adler, the only woman to outwit the master detective, as a sleuth in *Good Night, Mr. Holmes,* a *New York Times* Notable Book of the Year.

Carole exchanges deerstalker for cat ears to pen the popular Midnight Louie mysteries, a blend of traditional "cozy" and classic "noir" that offers both satire and substance. Set in a slightly surreal Las Vegas, the series features four human crime-solvers unknowingly aided by "Sam Spade with hairballs," a burly black alley cat. Midnight Louie's first-person-feline narrations thread through the novels, creating an underworld of animal characters.

How Carole Met Louie

It's been thirty years since the human/feline mystery writing team first laid eyes on one another. Carole was a feature writer intrigued by a long, thirty-dollar ad in the *St. Paul Pioneer Press* classifieds, offering one Midnight Louie to a good home for a dollar. The streetwise tomcat, "equally at home on your best couch as in your neighbor's garbage can" had been surviving splendidly at an upscale Palo Alto motel by eating the pond's huge, priceless koi. He also ankled up to female lodgers on chilly evenings to ensure a cozy crash pad for the night. A woman guest flew Louie home to St. Paul to save him from death at the local pound, but he languished in apartment living, so she advertised to find him a rural home where he could rule a more spacious roost. Letting Louie tell his story in his own words, Carole released a humorous and hard-boiled voice that combines Damon Runyon, generic gumshoe, and Mrs. Malaprop.

Eleven years later Carole and her husband, Sam Douglas, relocated to Fort Worth, Texas. The freshly full-time novelist was hunting a creative framing device for an innovative four-book romantic suspense series . . . Midnight Louie resurfaced to take the job. He now has twenty novels and many short stories behind him. Neither of them has ever looked back . . . although, when visiting H. P. Lovecraft country, one definitely should.